Martina Finds a Shiny Coin

A Loving Adaptation to the Folktale of Martina and Perez

To Ora Luz:

With much love –

12/15/18
@Artspace
NYC

Written by Yadhira Gonzalez-Taylor

Illustrated by Alba Escayo

Please refer to the glossary for translation of Spanish and Taino words.

IBSN-13: 978-1490436753

ISBN-10: 1490436758

Printed in the USA

For all the Martinas in the world.

For the residents of *El Barrio Borinquen Parcelas* in Caguas, Puerto Rico, for teaching me the meaning of community.

Many full moons ago, there was a little *cucarachita* named Martina. She lived in a little house in the middle of a tiny village called Borinquen. The village was surrounded by giant green mountains.

Martina loved to clean, sing, read, and play the cello. Every day she would wake up with the rooster's crow to scrub everything until it shined like gold. Then, she would read, play the cello, sing, or dance *bomba y plena*.

One morning, she was sweeping the *batey* when she found a shiny coin. She decided to save the coin in the little purse Grandmother Cucaracha had given her.

The next day, she woke up earlier than the rooster, and put on a colorful dress and *chancletas*. She scurried to *la guagua* stop as fast as she could. *La guagua* would get her to the *pueblo* to search for something special. Martina waited with a duck, a dog, a rat, and a goat. When *la guagua* came, they all took turns climbing on board.

Martina sat next to the driver so she could enjoy the view on the way to the *pueblo*. But, the loud chatter of the animals made Martina cover her ears. *The ride will not be fun with all this noise*, she thought. When they arrived at the *pueblo*, Martina gave the driver the shiny coin, and he gave her three *pesetas* in change.

Martina walked toward *las tiendas*. She admired the tropical trees, and looked at all the wonderful things for sale. She looked around, and thought about what she might buy. Would she buy new *sandalias*, or *zapatos*? Maybe a shirt, or ribbons for her antennae? She didn't quite know. There was too much to choose from

GLORIA

ZAPATOS
MEDIAS

Suddenly, Martina saw a sign in big blue letters that read La Casa de Las Chucherias. Outside, a giant palmetto bug yelled, "Come on in, cucarachas and cucarachones! We have knickknacks, dolls, games, household items, coats, shoes, and much more!"

When Martina entered the store, she found a beautiful *gata* behind the counter. "Good morning, I am *Señorita Gata Lucia*. May I help you?" she asked. "I have some money, and I am looking to buy something special," said Martina. *Señorita Gata Lucia* looked at her and said, "You have a good-looking face. But, I think you would look better with a little face powder. Also, if you hide your antennae under a *pañuelo*, you will look more like a girl and less like a roach." Martina looked at *Señorita Gata* and thought; *She must be right. After all, she does look beautiful with all those colors on her face.*

¡OLÉ!

"That will be two *pesetas*," said *La Gata* Lucia. Martina handed her two *pesetas*, and saved the last one to pay for the ride home. *La Gata* Lucia handed Martina a pretty little powder set that opened up like a music box. The set had a drawing of a lady wearing a beautiful red *flamenco* dress. Martina looked at herself in the mirror, took a little powder, and dabbed it on her face. "¡Olé! Now I will look like a *flamenco* dancer," she said. Martina scurried back to *la guagua*, hopped on, and sat quietly in the back. She imagined how beautiful she was going to be with her new look.

When Martina got home, she put on her best dress; the one that had butterflies, polka dots, and rainbows. She put on a new pair of *chancletas*, and dabbed on an enormous amount of face powder. She applied a little more lipstick, and hid her antennae under a *pañuelo*.

Martina, ran to the *balcón*, and sat on a rocking chair to read about butterflies, elephants, and circuses near and far. Suddenly, *El Gato* Ramon, the librarian from the *pueblo*, stopped and meowed, "Martina, how beautiful you look today! Even though you are a *cucarachita* and I am a *gato*, I would like to marry you.

Will you marry me?"

Martina looked at him and thought, *He must have noticed me when I went to the library to borrow books about butterflies, elephants, and circuses near and far. If I marry him, I can read at the library all day long.* Martina answered quickly, "I will marry you. But first, tell me what you like most about me?"

Señor Gato immediately answered, "All that face powder makes you look absolutely beautiful." Martina felt a little sad. She didn't want to marry someone who didn't care about her love of books. Martina looked at Señor Gato, and said, "I am afraid your meowing would keep me up at night. I cannot marry you." Señor Gato became embarrassed and said, "Well, you are a cucarachita after all. I don't think my friends would approve." He walked away, and never spoke to Martina again.

The next day, Martina put on more face powder, a little lipstick, and again hid her antennae under a *pañuelo*. She put on the same dress and *chancletas*. She grabbed her cello, and sat in the garden to play her favorite song, *Lamento Borincano* in D major.

Suddenly, *El Perro* Juan, the famous pianist appeared. He was wearing a beautiful *Guayabera* and a *fedora* hat. *Señor Perro* stopped and barked, "*Que bonita*, Martina. Even though you are a *cucarachita* and I am a *perro*, I am willing to marry you. Will you marry me?"

Martina looked at him, and thought, *If I marry him, I can play the cello while he plays the piano all day long.* "*Señor Perro*, I will marry you. But first, tell me what you like most about me?" she said. *Señor Perro*, eagerly wagging his tail said, "It is simple. I fell in love with your face with all that face powder."

Martina had hoped that he liked her for her music, and not for her beauty. "I am sorry, I can't marry you. Your bark is too loud and it scares me," she said. *Señor Perro* was highly offended. "How dare you?" he barked. "I am the best pianist ever! Very well then, I don't think a *perro* and a *cucarachita* would make much of a duet anyway." He left, dragging his tail behind him, and never came back.

Martina went inside her tiny house, and cried. *Señor Gato* and *Señor Perro* had noticed her for her face powder, not for her love of reading, or her musical skills. She thought that maybe if she sang loud, and clear, she might attract a true friend who would sing with her. She really loved to sing, and dance *bomba y plena*. All the insects and animals of Borinquen knew she was good at making songs up on the spot.

Martina woke up the next day, once again cleaned her house, put on some more face powder, more lipstick and hid her antennae. She put on the same dress, and went out to sweep the *batey*. She was sweeping, and singing *La Borinqueña*, when she heard a loud quack that made her jump. It was *El Pato* Roberto. "*¡No lo puedo creer! ¡Que bella!* Martina, marry me, I don't care that you are a *cucarachita* and I am a *pato*," he said.

"Hola, Señor Pato," said Martina. Señor Pato was a famous opera singer. If I marry him, I can travel the world, and sing with him, she thought. "Okay, I will marry you. But first, tell me what you like most about me?" asked Martina. "I have never seen such a beauty as you. You look more like a girl, and not so much like a cockroach," said Señor Pato. "Was there anything else that you noticed about me?" she asked. She hoped to hear that he loved her singing. "I just want to look at your face till the day I die!" he said.

"You mean you have never heard me sing, or play the cello? Did you know that I like to read books about butterflies, elephants, and circuses near and far?" asked Martina. "Who cares about that? I can pay someone to do that for you," said *Señor Pato*. "I am sorry, *Señor Pato*, I cannot marry you. Your quacking is too loud and hurts my tiny ears," said Martina. *Señor Pato* became very angry, and said, "I should have known better than to talk to a *cucarachita*." He wobbled away, quacking something rude under his breath.

That night, Martina cried, imagining the love of her life was tall, strong, and handsome. "Surely, he must exist somewhere. Surely, he has noticed me," she whispered as she sobbed.

The next day, Martina put on the same dress, some more face powder, and a little lipstick. She hid her antennae, and sat in the *balcón*, rocking back and forth. She closed her eyes, and pretended she was wearing a blue dress with hearts while her antennae moved freely in the warm and gentle Caribbean breeze. Martina pretended she was enjoying the view of the sun as it set on the water.

Suddenly, Martina heard a tiny sigh. This woke her from her imaginary trip to the beach. She heard it again; this time it sounded very sad. She thought it was an ant, or a ladybug, perhaps too small to be seen or heard. Then, she saw him, standing beyond the *batey*. It was a mouse, standing under a *flamboyan* tree, looking at Martina with a sad face. *El Ratón* Miguel was dressed like a *jíbaro*, his clothes were wrinkled, and he was wearing a *pava*. He looked like he was just back from cutting sugar cane at the *cañaveral*.

"May I help you?" said Martina, feeling bothered. *What can he want? He better not ask to marry me for my face like Perro, Gato, and Pato,* she thought. "No, you can't do much for me, Señorita. I am very sad today," said Miguel. "Oh, come on, just tell me what the problem is, or leave," said Martina, rushing him along. The mouse began to cry, and said, "Well, you see, my fine young lady, every day for the past year I have walked by and admired a beautiful *cucarachita* that lives in this house."

The mouse continued to cry and explained, "Sometimes she is playing the cello. Other times she is singing beautiful songs about Borinquen. I have seen her reading my favorite type of books about butterflies, elephants, and circuses near and far. She is the most beautiful creature I have ever seen. I finally got enough courage to give her a *serenata* of love songs, but when I got here, I only saw you. One day you were talking to a snooty *gato*. The next day I came back, and saw you talking to a loud *perro*, then to an angry *pato*. I have not seen my beautiful *cucarachita* ever again! I am afraid I have lost her forever," said Miguel.

Martina could not believe her ears. Here was this *ratoncito jíbaro*, in love with her for who she was, and not the powder on her face. Martina told the mouse to wait one second, and ran inside the house to wash her face. She changed her dress, and removed the *pañuelo*. She ran back to the *batey*, and said, "*¡Hola!* My name is Martina! What's your name?"

Miguel could not believe his eyes. His beloved had been in the house all along. "Martina!" squeaked the mouse. "What a beautiful name. My name is Miguel, and I have loved you since the first day I saw you.

You were inside the house the whole time? You are so beautiful, smart, and talented. Will you marry me?" Martina thought about *Gato*, *Perro*, and *Pato*. She realized they all loved her for one thing, her beauty. Here, this *ratoncito* loved her for who she was, and what she loved. "Of course I will marry you Miguel," said Martina.

By the next full moon, they were married and spent their first days as mouse and roach under two coconut trees, swinging together in a comfy *hamaca*. After that, they lived happily ever after in the enchanted village of Borinquen, in a tiny mouse, surrounded by giant green mountains.

Glossary

Balcón: Balcony or veranda

Batey: A Taino (Arawak) indigenous word meaning the front yard to a home or ceremonial meeting grounds, made of red clay.

Bomba y Plena: *Bomba* is the traditional Afro-Caribbean music of Puerto Rico, where the dancer leads the drums with his or her movements. *Plena* is also traditional Puerto Rican music which contains more of a Spanish influence.

Cañaveral: Sugar plantation

Chancletas: Flip-flop styled shoes or sandals

Cucaracha: Grown female cockroach

Cucarachita: Young or small female cockroach

Cucarachones: Grown male cockroaches

El Gato: The male cat

Fedora: A tropical hat

Flamboyan: Flamboyant tree

Flamenco: Music or dance from Spain

Guayabera: A tropical shirt

Hola: Hello or greetings

Jíbaro: A male who lives in the mountainous regions of the island of Puerto Rico. Traditionally, a farmer in the coffee, sugar cane, or tobacco plantations.

La Borinqueña: The official anthem of the Commonwealth of Puerto Rico

La Casa de Las Chucherías: The House of Knickknacks

La Gata: The female cat

La Guagua: The passenger van, a traditional mode of public transport in Puerto Rico from rural areas to town areas.

La Hamaca: The hammock

Las Tiendas: The stores

Medias: Socks

No lo Puedo Creer: I cannot believe it.

¡Olé!: Spanish expression uttered during flamenco dancing or bull fighting. Also, used to express general excitement, or encouragement.

Lamento Borincano: A song titled, Lament of Borinquen, describing the difficulties of being a hard working *jíbaro* of limited economic means.

Pañuelo: Handkerchief suitable for head covering

Pato: Male duck

Pava: A traditional straw hat

Perro: Male dog

Pesetas: Quarter (U.S. dollar) or coin

Pueblo: Town

Que Bella: How beautiful

Que Bonita: How pretty

Ratón: Mouse

Ratoncito: Little or young mouse

Sandalias: Sandals

Señor: Sir or Mr.

Señorita: A young lady who has never been married

Serenata: A romantic suitor's love songs to his beloved, normally accompanied by others playing instruments

Zapatos: shoes

Dear Reader,

Thank you for reading this book about *la cucarachita* Martina, and her search for something special. The place described in this book is real. *El Barrio Borinquen, sector Parcelas Viejas,* is located in rural Caguas, Puerto Rico. *Las Parcelas Viejas* houses a population of approximately 800 people, and is surrounded by lush green trees, giant mountains, and wild plant and animal life. Martina's little house was inspired by a house everyone calls *La Tienda Grande* (the big store). Once upon a time it was a store, but now serves as a nunnery. It is over 100 years old, and it was one of the first structures built when that area was settled by people working in the sugar, and tobacco plantations.

I spent some of the best years of my life in *Las Parcelas Viejas*. This is where I fell in love for the first time, ran around with friends, escaped to the top of the mountains to visit the waterfalls, and swam in the river during hot summer days. My grandparents and I sold Avon products, door to door. I always remember how the people in my tiny paradise loved each other, and always shared what they had. Some people even grew, and still grow, vegetables and fruits in their tiny parcels to share with neighbors. To me, *Parcelas Viejas* is a magical place where love stories like Martina's can happen. It is a place where true beauty is obvious to the one who seeks it.

I hope if you ever visit Puerto Rico, also known as The Enchanted Island, you will stop by the house where Martina and Miguel "live" happily ever after. Thank you for purchasing or borrowing this book. I hope you and your loved ones enjoyed it and will share Martina's story with others.

Sincerely,

Yadhira Gonzalez-Taylor, Esq.

For more information about Caguas, Puerto Rico,
visit the following websites:

http://www.visitacaguas.com

http://www.pr.gov

http://www.topuertorico.org

http://www.seepuertorico.com

Visit Martina on Facebook at

www.facebook.com/martinafindsashinycoin

Made in the USA
Lexington, KY
14 April 2018